Dear mouse friends,
Welcome to the world of

Geronimo Stilton

THE RODENT'S GAZETTE
EDITORIAL STAFF

Geronimo Stilton
A learned and brainy
mouse; editor of
The Rodent's Gazette

Thea Stilton
Geronimo's sister and
special correspondent at
The Rodent's Gazette

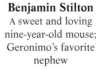

Trap Stilton
An awful joker;
Geronimo's cousin and
owner of the store
Cheap Junk for Less

Benjamin Stilton
A sweet and loving
nine-year-old mouse;
Geronimo's favorite
nephew

Geronimo Stilton

THE HUNT FOR THE GOLDEN BOOK

PLUS a bonus Mini Mystery and cheesy jokes!

WITHDRAWN

Scholastic Inc.

ISBN 978-0-545-64649-9

Pages i–111; 194–214 copyright © 2010 by Edizioni Piemme S.p.A., Corso Como 15, 20154 Milan, Italy.

Pages 112–193 copyright © 2007 by Edizioni Piemme S.p.A.

International Rights © Atlantyca S.p.A.

Pages i–111; 194–214 English translation © 2014 by Atlantyca S.p.A.

Pages 112–193 English translation © 2012 by Atlantyca S.p.A

Based on an original idea by Elisabetta Dami.
www.geronimostilton.com

Published by Scholastic Inc., 557 Broadway, New York, NY 10012. SCHOLASTIC and associated logos are trademarks and/or registered trademarks of Scholastic Inc.

Stilton is the name of a famous English cheese. It is a registered trademark of the Stilton Cheese Makers' Association. For more information, go to www.stiltoncheese.com.

Pages i–111
Text by Geronimo Stilton
Original title *Caccia al libro d'oro*
Cover by Silvia Bigolin
Illustrations by Danilo Barozzi and Silvia Bigolin (design) and Christian Aliprandi (color)
Graphics by Chiara Cebraro

Pages 112–193
Text by Geronimo Stilton
Original title *Il mostro di Lago Lago*
Illustrations by Claudio Cernuschi (pencils and ink) and Giuseppe Di Dio (color)
Graphics by Michela Battaglin and Marta Lorini
Fingerprint graphic © NREY/Shutterstock

Special thanks to Shannon Penney and Beth Dunfey
Translated by Lidia Morson Tramontozzi and Julia Heim
Interior design by Theresa Venezia and Becky James

12 11 10 9 8 7 6 5 4 3 2 1   14 15 16 17 18/0

Printed in the U.S.A.   23

First printing, March 2014

TABLE OF CONTENTS

Geronimo Stilton

THE HUNT FOR THE GOLDEN BOOK

Scholastic Inc.

A Mountain of Books!

It all started one peaceful evening. . . .

I was **dusting** my bookcase at home, happy as a mouse in a vat of fondue. I had finally decided to tidy up the shelves where I keep the special $\boxed{F}\boxed{I}\boxed{R}\boxed{S}\boxed{T}$ $\boxed{E}\boxed{D}\boxed{I}\boxed{T}\boxed{I}\boxed{O}\boxed{N}\boxed{S}$ of all the books I've written. But I hadn't cleaned in such a long time that a thick cloud of **dust** formed around my head. Rats! I began to sneeze like crazy.

Achoo!

"**ACHOO! ACHOO! AAAAAAACHOO!**"

Oops, I'm sorry — I haven't introduced myself! My name is Stilton, *Geronimo Stilton*. I run *The Rodent's Gazette*, the most famouse newspaper on Mouse Island, but the thing that makes me squeak with joy is writing **ADVENTURE** stories!

Now, where was I? Oh, right — I was getting rid of the dust on the bookcase when I began to sneeze so hard that I lost my balance. Holey cheese! I grabbed on to the bookcase to steady myself, and it **toPPLeD** forward. **EVERY** book, and I mean **every** single book on **EVERY** shelf, fell smack on my head.

Squeak!

YOUCH! THAT HURT!

Heeeeeeeelp!

As I climbed out from under the **MOUNTAIN** of books, something suddenly struck me. (And it wasn't another book!) I realized that exactly **TEN YEARS** had passed since I started publishing my adventures! After my first book, I just kept writing **more** and **more** and **more**. . . .

During those **TEN YEARS**, I published more than **seventy-five books** . . . and all **seventy-five** of them had just fallen right on top of me. Moldy mozzarella!

Even though my head was throbbing, I looked at the **MOUNTAIN** of books and sighed happily. I have to confess, I'm a very *sentimental* rodent!

Ten years . . .

Just then, the phone RANG. It was my cousin Trap.

"Hey there, Gerrykins! Where's the PARTY?"

Maybe I'd been hit on the head harder than I'd thought — I had **NO IDEA** what he was squeaking about. "What party?" I asked.

"Germeister, you're a real CHEESEHEAD sometimes! The party at *The Rodent's Gazette*, of course! I invited all my friends!"

I frowned. "First of all, my name is not Gerrykins or Germeister. And second, I'm not throwing a party for your **friends**!"

"Gerry Berry, you're such a PARTY POOPER! Just let me know when you figure it out. I'm already DROOLING just thinking about all the fabumouse food!" He hung up.

Just as I put the phone down, it RANG AGAIN. *Squeak!*

This time, it was Sally Ratmousen, one of

my least favorite mice. She grumbled, "Stilton, I heard you're having a P∧R☆Y at *The Rodent's Gazette*. SHOWING OFF, huh?"

SALLY RATMOUSEN
Editor of
The Daily Rat

I tried to stay as cool as a mozzarella milkshake. "I'm not having a party, Sally."

"You'd better not be, Stilton, OR ELSE. . . ." She hung up without another word.

My whiskers TREMBLED. Putrid cheese puffs, Sally is one mean mouse!

The phone RANG AGAIN. Cheese and crackers, this was getting ridiculous! My sister, Thea, was on the line. "Geronimo, you've taken care of everything for next week's P∧R☆Y, right?"

EMBARRASSED, I answered, "Well, actually . . . no! What are we celebrating?"

Thea groaned. "Come on, Geronimo! It's been TEN YEARS since you started writing your adventures. We're throwing an enormouse PARTY to celebrate. Just about everyone in New Mouse City is invited!"

I had to admit, I liked the idea of CELEBRATING all my books — but I'm not a mouse who likes to be the center of attention. I promised Thea I'd think about it and headed to bed.

To party . . . or not to party?

Swiss cheese on rye, I was **exhausted**! Little did I know that it would be my last peaceful night for a long time. . . .

RING! RING! RIIIIIIIIING!

The next morning at exactly five o'clock, the phone started ringing again.

RING! RIIING! RIIIIIIIIING!

I answered with my eyes half-open.

Hello?

"Hello? This is Stilton, *Geronimo Stilton*," I squeaked sleepily.

A familiar voice **BOOMED** in my ear.

"Grandson, I know who you are. Stop wasting time! I need you to come to *The Rodent's Gazette* immediately. It's an **EMERGENCY**!"

It was my grandfather William Shortpaws, aka Cheap Mouse Willie. He's the **founder** of *The Rodent's Gazette*, which he points out at least once a day! I had no choice but to **GET UP** and take care of the emergency. There's no arguing with my grandfather! I **SPRINTED** out of the house in my pajamas and slippers and ran down the street as **FAST** as my paws would take me.

When I got to *The Rodent's Gazette*, I was huffing and puffing like a **Steam engine**. My grandfather was waiting in **MY** office, sitting in **MY** chair with his paws on **MY** desk.

Argh!

As soon as he saw me, Grandfather William clicked his **STOPWATCH** and bellowed, **"Not good, not good at all!** It took you eight minutes and forty-eight seconds to get here. I said '*immediately*,' and when I say '*immediately*,' I mean *immediately*! Understand?"

I tried to catch my breath. "But, Grandfather, I came as fast as I could. . . ."

My grandfather PEERED at me through

his tiny, silver-rimmed glasses and boomed, "**Not good, not good at all!** You're still in your pajamas! You haven't brushed your teeth or combed your whiskers! And I bet you haven't even eaten breakfast! This is not how you come to the office, Grandson."

I scuffed one of my slippers on the cheese-colored carpet. "But, Grandfather, it's five o'clock in the morning! I'm usually still asleep. And I haven't had breakfast because you told me it was an emergency!" At that moment, my stomach growled.

He continued, "**Not good, not good at all!** Breakfast is the most important meal of the day. When I was your age, I would have been in the office for hours by now! Go make yourself PRESENTABLE."

I SLIPPED into the bathroom. In five minutes flat, I had washed my paws and face,

Brush, brush, brush . . .

Done!

Ready!

Yummy!

brushed my teeth, combed my fur, and changed into the suit I keep at *The Rodent's Gazette* for EMERGENCIES. (I tend to make a MESS of myself with cheese smoothies!) Then I went to the vending machine and pressed the SUPER ENERGY BOOSTER AGED CHEESE SMOOTHIE WITH WHIPPED CREAM AND SUGAR button. **(YUMMY!)** After that, I pressed the LARGE CREAM-CHEESE-AND-PEAR TART button. **(YUM, YUM, YUM!)** Sometimes listening to Grandfather William isn't so bad!

After GOBBLING breakfast in two shakes of a mouse's tail,

I headed back to my office.

When my grandfather saw me, he barely **RAISED** his eyes from the desk and squeaked, "It's about time! Next Saturday is the **big** party at *The Rodent's Gazette*. It's been **TEN YEARS** since you started writing books! We need to start scheduling **interviews**, TV appearances, and the party itself, of course."

I interrupted him. My whiskers were **wobbling**.

"What did you say? Grandfather, I'm getting stressed just thinking about it! You know that I'm a **shy mouse**. I really don't want a party at all!"

I expected my grandfather to **YELL** at me, or get angry, or maybe try to force me into it somehow. But instead . . .

INSTEAD, A STRANGE THING HAPPENED:

1 Suddenly his shoulders drooped . . .

2 His whiskers began to tremble . . .

5 He blew his nose on my tie . . .

6 And dried his eyes on my sleeve!

4 And he began to cry like a baby!

3 His eyes filled with tears . . .

8 By then, I didn't know what to do!

7 Then he started to beg. . . .

OH, LOLA!

Grandfather William flooded my office with TEARS.

"Grandson, I'm desperate! You have to help me! You wouldn't say no to the **GRANDFATHER** who loves you so much that he put you in charge of *The Rodent's Gazette,* would you?"

Seeing him like that, I couldn't help getting TEARY-EYED. I'm such a softy!

I reassured him. "Grandfather, you know that I *love* you, too. How can I help you? I'll do anything!"

A glimmer of **SATISFACTION** flashed in his eyes and he quickly asked, "You'll **help** me? Give me your word, Geronimo!"

I nodded. "Of course, I give you my word. Now please stop *BLOWING* your nose on my tie!"

My grandfather immediately stopped his CRYING, straightened his shoulders, and rubbed his hands together with GLEE. "Good, very good. Here's what I need done. . . ."

He stuck a list under my snout that was at least a mile long. **Thundering cat tails!** I read it out loud.

TO DO FOR THE PARTY:

1. **ORGANIZE** A HUGE BASH! DON'T WORRY ABOUT THE COST. IT MUST BE **LUXURIOUS, CLASSY,** AND **ELABORATE.**

2. **INVITE** ALL THE MOST FAMOUSE RODENTS IN NEW MOUSE CITY (**ESPECIALLY** COUNTESS LOLA VON MUENSTER) AND ALL OF THE REPORTERS ON MOUSE ISLAND (ESPECIALLY SALLY RATMOUSEN SO SHE CAN SEE HOW SUCCESSFUL WE ARE), AND SPARE NO EXPENSE!

3. **TELL GERONIMO TO WRITE** AND PUBLISH A SPECIAL BOOK WITH A BEAUTIFUL GOLDEN COVER. IN THIS BOOK, HE'LL EXPLAIN THAT HE BECAME AN AUTHOR **BECAUSE OF ME!** THAT HE LEARNED EVERYTHING HE KNOWS FROM ME! THAT HIS SUCCESS IS ALL BECAUSE OF ME! IN OTHER WORDS . . . EVERYTHING IS BECAUSE OF ME!

I was about to EXPLODE like the fireworks at New Mouse City's Fourth of July celebration. I'd fallen for Grandfather William's trick like a mouse in a trap — again!

Grandfather cheerfully PINCHED my cheek.

"Don't get your tail in a twist, Geronimo! The SPECIAL book you'll write for the occasion is guaranteed to sell *millions* of copies. Plus, that jealous Sally Ratmousen will finally have to acknowledge all the wonderful things we've **accomplished** through the years! Doesn't that make you happy?"

I finally did EXPLODE.

"No, I'm not happy! I don't like PARTIES! And I don't think it's a good idea to invite Sally. She'll be mad, and then who knows what she'll do to get EVEN." My whiskers twitched at the thought. "And I don't even know who *Countess Lola* is!"

Super Scoop

Countess Lola in New Mouse City!

Countess Lola von Muenster will be visiting our city this week. She's sure to make all social events that she attends extra-fabumouse!

GRANDFATHER WILLIAM'S TINY TEAR

Grandfather pulled out the latest edition of *Rat Chat*, New Mouse City's most popular **gossip** newspaper, and stuck it under my snout.

PUZZLED, I read the article and asked, "But what does Countess Lola have to do with the party at *The Rodent's Gazette*?"

My grandfather suddenly **blushed**.

"Well . . . when I was younger, the countess and I went to school together. She was very *beautiful*, very **charming**, very smart, very **rich**, very **famouse**, and from a very **noble** family!" Grandfather William twirled his whiskers, embarrassed. "I . . . ahem . . . had a terrible crush on her, like everyone else in the school, but she never even bothered to **LOOK** at me. She didn't think I was worthy of her!" He sat up and straightened his tie. "But now I can **WIN** her heart. I'm a successful mouse, and founder of *The Rodent's Gazette*!"

I sighed. "Ah, love! Grandfather, I didn't think you were the romantic type." I picked up the phone and handed it to him. "Go ahead, call Countess Lola! Invite her out to dinner, and send her a bouquet of yellow roses, the color of cheese . . . or tiny chocolate-covered cheeses in a **HEART-SHAPED BOX** . . . . You could even add a nice romantic note to tell her you've always loved her . . . ."

My grandfather moaned, "No, no, no, I can't! What if I get rejected again? You have to help me **impress** her with this party! Remember, Geronimo — you gave me your word!"

Then he sighed, and a little TEAR slowly slid down his snout. "Oh, Lola . . . "

I put down the phone and quickly handed him my handkerchief before he **BLEW HIS NOSE** on my tie again. Slimy Swiss cheese, that was gross!

"Okay, Grandfather, I'll **help** you," I said with a sigh. "But not because I got tricked into giving you my word. I'll help you because I'm a mouse who believes in *true love!*"

WRITE! WRITE! WRITE!

Grandfather finally GRINNED.

"Here's my plan," he said, suddenly as *happy* as a mouse in a swimming pool of Swiss cheese. "Lola is a big fan of yours, so she'll surely come to the party. We must make sure that it is FANCY and **fabumouse**! You'll write a new book for the occasion, which will explain that your SUCCESS as a writer is all because of me. That's the TRUTH after all! Then Lola will finally see what an accomplished, influential mouse I am, and she'll fall madly in *love* with me."

By now, Grandfather had a huge smile across his snout. He slapped my back hard enough to flatten a GORILLA and boomed, "Enough chitchat. The party is only a week away! WRITE! WRITE! WRITE!"

He dashed out the door, slamming it behind him.

Finally, some peace and quiet!

I TURNED to walk toward my desk, but my **JACKET** was caught in the door. It pulled me back like a rubber band! I BANGED my head hard against the door and fainted.

When I finally came to, it was already late morning. Rat-munching rattlesnakes, there wasn't a second to waste!

I threw open the door and **SHOUTED**, "Emergency meeting!"

Ouch!

There was panic in the newsroom.

Priscilla Prettywhiskers shouted, "**WHat? An emergency?** Do you want me to **CALL** the doctor? The firemice? Your sister? Your cousin Trap? Tina Spicytail? **Your grandfather?**"

I held up a paw. I couldn't hear myself think!

"Definitely not my grandfather! But please call Tina right away. I **NEED** a pan of lasagna with **triple cheese** to keep me going!"

I headed back into my office, but then turned and added, "And most important, don't call my grandfather — **for any reason!**"

Patty Plumprat leaped up on her desk and squeaked, "Hurry, everyone! It's an **EMERGENCY!**"

Cheesita de la Pampa jumped up so fast that she fell on the floor and **BRUISED** her tail. She even **spilled** her warm banana cheese smoothie on her computer keyboard!

Gigi Gogo slipped a pen behind an ear, grabbed a notebook, and squeaked, "**I'm ready**, Geronimo!"

An instant later, Tina ran in with an **ENORMOUSE** steaming pan of lasagna. My mouth started watering like a sprinkler on a hot day. My cousin

Lasagna for everyone!

TINA SPICYTAIL
Grandfather William's trusted housekeeper

Trap followed close behind Tina, shouting, "**YUM, TIME FOR SOME LASAGNA!**"

Just then, the roar of an engine filled the newsroom.

VROOOOOOOOOOM! VROOOOOOOOOOOOOOM!

My sister, Thea, zoomed in on her motorcycle and skidded to a **stop** less than two whiskers away from my chair. She took off her helmet and said, "Here I am! I heard there was an EMERGENCY. What's up, Geronimo?"

I tried to answer, but I was so wound up that my whiskers were TREMBLING, my paws were sweating, my heart was POUNDING, and my tongue was **dry**. I was a mess!

Priscilla calmed me down by waving cheese-scented smelling salts under my snout. Mmm!

After a moment, I stopped drooling and finally found the **strength** to say, "Friends, next Saturday there's going to be a big PARTY at *The Rodent's Gazette* to celebrate my TENTH ANNIVERSARY as an author of books!"

Everyone murmured with excitement, but I held up a paw. "For this special occasion, my grandfather has forced — um — *asked* me to write and publish a NEW BOOK with a gold cover. But . . ." I paused. "We only have seven days to do it! WE'LL NEVER MAKE IT!"

Missy McSlice grabbed a calculator and began clicking away.

"Hmm . . . for a SPECIAL occasion like this, we don't

MISSY MCSLICE
Geronimo's loyal advisor

have to pinch pennies!" She grinned. "Let's not look at the expenses. Why don't we make this cover special and shiny? I already have a mouserific idea for the title. We could call it THE GOLDEN BOOK!"

Everyone cheered. "Two paws up for THE GOLDEN BOOK!"

When they quieted down, I noticed that Patty Plumprat was frowning. "But who's going to print THE GOLDEN BOOK on such short notice?"

HOW A BOOK IS MADE

After an author writes a fabumouse story, he or she submits it to a publisher. If the publisher likes it, the book is signed up and the text is revised by an editor (and sometimes illustrated by an artist). Once the text and images are finished, a designer lays out the pages with everything in the right place. Finally, the files are delivered to the printer to be printed and bound, and the finished books are delivered to stores to be sold!

Missy exclaimed, "I have an **IDEA** — let's call Frank Fastmouse! He's the most famous **PROBLEM SOLVER** in New Mouse City!"

Before I could shake a paw, a gray-furred rodent with deep blue eyes burst into the room. He wore an *elegant* suit with a stylish **pinstriped** shirt and a tie the color of cheddar cheese. (I almost began to drool at the thought of cheese. Rats, was I hungry!)

I squeaked, "**MR. FASTMOUSE**, please help us! Please, I **beg** you, think of something! Anythiiiiiiing!"

Help us!

FRANK FASTMOUSE
New Mouse City's
most famous
problem solver

Frank smiled, stepped to the side, and mumbled into his cell phone. When he hung up, he said, "**Problem solved!** I know a printer in Mouseport, called **SUPER** (which stands for 'Super-Ultra-Precise and Extremely Rapid') **Print**. They work day and **NIGHT**. Send them the text and illustrations for the new book when they're ready, and SUPER Print will **IMMEDIATELY** return the printed pages, bound together as books."

Everyone cheered.

Amazed, I wiped the sweat off my snout and thanked him. "But how did you do it?" I asked.

Frank bowed and smiled mysteriously. "Oh, I didn't do anything *special*. I'm just one mouse. But when we all work together, we are **STRONG — VERY STRONG**!"

He nodded at me and said, "Now it's up to you, Mr. Stilton. Here's my advice: Start writing the book right now. WRITE! WRITE! WRITE! And don't stop until it's finished!"

Rotten rat's teeth, that sounded just like what Grandfather William had said!

My coworkers all shouted together, "WRITE! WRITE! WRITE, GERONIMO!"

I thanked them from the bottom of my heart, waved, and went back into my office. I pulled a SIGN from my desk drawer.

PLEASE DO NOT DISTURB! WRITING IN PROGRESS!

I only use the sign in true emergencies. Normally, my office door is always open!

IS THAT HIM?
IT CAN'T BE!

I sat at my desk and opened my trusty laptop, which greeted me with its usual sound: **DING!**

I stared at the blank screen, waiting for inspiration to strike so that I could start writing *The Golden Book*.

I stared and stared and stared . . . but I was struck with nothing.

Nothing.

No inspiration.

My mind was blank.

Totally blank.

I stared at the computer for a long time, getting more and more desperate. After a while, I felt like **tearing** out my whiskers!

Suddenly, I remembered a **FAMOUSE**

Mouse Island saying:

Nothing is more inspiring than cheese for lunch!

Since it was lunchtime, I decided to look for inspiration in the place that inspires me most: **Sir Squeaks**, the best gourmet cheese shop in New Mouse City.

A few hours later (whoops!), after I had been inspired by tiny tastes of fresh mozzarella balls, teensy tastes of fresh cheese slices, and huge tastes of some of the finest aged cheese around, I gobbled down **THREE** chocolate–blue cheese puffs, **FOUR** delicious ricotta tarts, and **THREE** servings of tiramisu.

(Okay, so maybe I went a little overboard.)

MOZZARELLA BALLS

HARD AND SOFT CHEESES

CHOCOLATE– BLUE CHEESE PUFFS

RICOTTA TARTS

TIRAMISU

After all that, I felt deliciously inspired!

Rubbing my **full** belly, I turned and I saw a rodent come into the shop. He had a **COMMANDING** presence, with short gray fur and **BEADY EYES** behind tiny glasses. Chewy cheese bits! That mouse looked a lot like *Grandfather William*!

But something didn't seem right.

There was a beautiful pink *orchid* in the buttonhole of his jacket, and he wore a *fancy* hat. But strangest of all was the unmistakable scent of Eau de Camembert (the favorite cologne of all the most *charming* rodents) that he left behind as he walked. . . .

STUNNED, I ducked behind my menu and watched him approach the counter. He picked out a PINK heart-shaped box of tiny PINK chocolates filled with PINK cream cheese with swirly PINK frosting on top. I had never seen so much PINK

in my life. There was no way that mouse could be my Grandfather William!

Just then, he turned toward me.

"**Grandson**, there's no use hiding behind the menu — I can see you! Why aren't you in your office writing? Get back there, you lazy lollygagger! WRITE! WRITE! WRITE!"

Cheese niblets, there was no mistaking him now!

It's Geronimo Stilton!

All the rodents packed in the bakery stared at me and MURMURED, "Isn't that Geronimo Stilton?"

"Did you hear that? He's LAZY!"

"He should be **writing** instead of gorging himself on mozzarella morsels!"

Blushing from the tip of my snout to the tip of my tail, I paid my bill and SCURRIED back to the office as fast as my paws would take me.

I felt like such a cheesebrain!

So I sat down and began to write again. Luckily, my full belly had given me lots of tasty inspiration. My fingers flew over the K E Y B O A R D as fast as the fingers of Cheddar O'Key, the most famouse pianist on Mouse Island!

But at that VERY moment, RIGHT when I was beginning to think that maybe I could actually finish writing THE GOLDEN BOOK in time, my phone rang.

It was *Grandfather William* — again! "Grandson, what are you doing?"

"I'm trying to write, just like you told me to —"

"TERRIFIC!" he boomed. "I just wanted to make sure you weren't still out there stuffing your belly with cheese pastries! **REMEMBER**, you gave me your word that you'd finish that book in time for the party."

I rolled my eyes. "Yes, believe me, I remember! Now I need to get back to it. There's not much time, and if you want to make a good impression on *Lola* —"

Grandfather William cut me off. "Speaking of Lola, what did you think of my NEW LOOK?"

"Oh, I — I don't know. . . ." I stammered. I couldn't tell him that I'd hardly recognized him!

"You were speechless, right?" he cried. "It's all thanks to Monsieur le Rat at the Chic Paws

Beauty Salon. I made an **APPOINTMENT** for you, too! You really need it, Grandson, with all the interviews and photo shoots you'll be doing to celebrate the TENTH ANNIVERSARY of your books. Aren't you **excited**? Monsieur le Rat says that you're a HOPELESS case, but he loves a challenge. He's already planning a **crash** beauty treatment for you!"

My tail twitched and my fur stood on end. "No, thank you!" I squeaked. "I have way too much to do — like writing THE GOLDEN BOOK!"

But before I could say anything else, Grandfather William had already hung up. Putrid cheese puffs, he was a stubborn mouse!

I thought about RUNNING AWAY, but

just then, someone knocked at my door. It was
Monsieur le Rat! He grabbed me by my tail
and dragged me to his *beauty salon*. Before
I had time to think, he began a complicated
beauty treatment on me.

He gave me a cucumber-and-gorgonzola-cheese
cleansing mask (**stinky!**), he shampooed
my fur with concentrated
Brie extract (**veeery**

Monsieur le Rat's
Chic Paws Beauty Salon
for the Sophisticated
Rodent

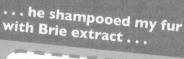
... he shampooed my fur
with Brie extract ...

Perfect!

He gave me a cucumber-
and-gorgonzola-cheese
cleansing mask ...

Voilà!

stinky!), he massaged me with sulfur-and-Limburger-cheese lotion (**extremely stinky!**), and he applied a cheddar-and-garlic nutrient mask for my stressed whiskers (the **stinkiest thing in the world!**).

So much for beauty treatments! When I got back to the office, I was such a rancid rodent that no one even wanted to come near me!

A little massage!

3

... he massaged me with sulfur-and-Limburger-cheese lotion ...

... and finally he applied a cheddar-and-garlic nutrient mask!

4

So stinky!

DIDN'T I TELL YOU NOT TO FALL ASLEEP?

As soon as I sat back down at my desk, my grandfather called again.

"Geronimo, enough relaxation!" he hollered. "You have to write *The Golden Book*! WRITE! WRITE! WRITE! AND DON'T FALL ASLEEP!"

I couldn't believe my ears. I'd been trying to write all day!

Grandfather William went on. "I'm giving you a bREaK by planning *The Rodent's Gazette* party myself. Satisfied?"

Whew, what a relief!

I worked through the NIGHT. By five o'clock the next morning, I crashed facedown on the keyboard.

I had been asleep for no more than five minutes when I woke up with a squeak. My grandfather threw open my office door and hollered, "Geronimo, are you sleeping? **DIDN'T I TELL YOU NOT TO FALL ASLEEP?** Now show me what you've written so far, lazybones!"

I grumbled, "Grandfather, I worked all night!" With a touch of *pride*, I shoved a printed-out draft of **THE GOLDEN BOOK** under his snout. By now, it was almost finished!

Grandfather sat in **MY** chair, put his paws on **MY** desk, grabbed **MY** red pen, straightened his tiny glasses on his nose . . . and began scribbling horrible **RED MARKS** all over the first page!

This is what my work looked like when he was **FINISHED** with it:

Dear mouse friends,

First of all, let me introduce myself. My name is

Stilton, Geronimo Stilton. I was born in New

THANKS TO MY AMAZING GRANDFATHER WILLIAM,

Mouse City, Mouse Island, and received a degree

in Mousomorphic Literature and Neo-Ratonic

Comparative Philosophy. For the past twenty

years, I have been running *The Rodent's Gazette*,

WHICH WAS FOUNDED BY MY ENTERPRISING AND INTELLIGENT GRANDFATHER —

New Mouse City's most widely read daily newspaper.

I have been awarded the Ratitzer Prize for my scoops

on *The Curse of the Cheese Pyramid* and *The Search*

— JUST TWO OF MANY ADVENTURES FUNDED AND SUPPORTED BY GRANDFATHER WILLIAM SHORTPAWS, OF COURSE

for Sunken Treasure. I also received the Andersen

2000 Prize for Personality of the Year.

In my spare time, I collect antique cheese rinds

from the seventh century, but my real passion is

— ADVENTURES WHICH WOULD NOT HAVE BEEN POSSIBLE WITHOUT THE LOVE AND HELP OF MY DEAR GRANDFATHER

writing books about my amazing adventures.

IN OTHER WORDS, I OWE IT ALL TO MY GRANDFATHER WILLIAM SHORTPAWS!

When Grandfather finished editing the book, there wasn't a single line without a RED MARK. Whiskers trembling with frustration, I cried, "Grandfather, you **changed** everything!"

Peering at me over his glasses, he answered CALMLY, "Geronimo, if you didn't have me to help, what would you do?"

"Some help you are!" I squeaked. "Now I have to rewrite it!"

He bolted out of the office *FASTER* than a mouse on a cheese hunt, yelling over his shoulder, "Now get your tail in gear! This book has to be **PERFECT** if I'm going to win Lola's heart!"

Dejected, I slumped back behind my desk. I ordered a HOT double mozzarella smoothie and continued working. I was so tired that the circles under my eyes turned as *PURPLE* as my friend Creepella von Cacklefur's cape.

I was sipping my SMOOTHIE when,

suddenly, I noticed a **note** in the cup. For the love of cheese, what could it be?

I unrolled it, **SHOOK** it off, and read the message. It was from my **SECRET-AGENT** friend,

Kornelius von Kickpaw (also known as OOK)!

STAY ALERT AND KEEP YOUR EYES WIDE OPEN!

YOUR FRIEND,
OOK

OOK

NAME: Kornelius von Kickpaw

CODE NAME: OOK

PROFESSION: Secret agent for the government of Mouse Island

WHO HE IS: Geronimo Stilton's friend from elementary school

SPECIAL QUALITIES: He always wears a trench coat and sunglasses — even at night!

FUN FACTS: He uses the craziest methods of warning and sending Geronimo messages — like putting a note in his smoothie!

HE ALWAYS FEARS THAT HIS MESSAGES WILL BE INTERCEPTED.

Kornelius von Kickpaw always leaves me the most MYSTERIOUS messages!

What did this one mean?

Why did I have to keep my EYES wide open?

I had learned to take Kornelius's WARNINGS seriously, so I tried to keep my eyes wide open the entire day. But since I had hardly slept the night before, I finally couldn't hold up my snout for another second! I fell fast asleep on top of my computer. . . .

I TOLD YOU TO KEEP YOUR EYES WIDE OPEN!

I woke up an hour later with an enormouse **BUMP** in the middle of my forehead. It was so big that I had to put a **BANDAGE** on it. Youch, that hurt!

How did I get that **LUMP**, anyway?

I couldn't remember. . . .

All I could remember was that because of my grandfather, Lola, and *The Golden Book*, I hadn't slept in my bed in days!

CHEESE NIBLETS, I WAS EXHAUSTED! TOTALLY EXHAUSTED!

In fact, I was so tired that I probably conked out on my C O M P U T E R and gave myself the big lump on my forehead.

But I remembered that I had done a really **good job**! I had made up for lost time, corrected everything Grandfather William wanted, and recycled the previous version. And now I was almost finished writing THE GOLDEN BOOK. After one last look, I could pass it along for printing.

HOLEY CHEESE, I had done it!

Suddenly, it hit me: If I had DENTED my

forehead, I had probably also dented my computer. Whoops! But when I looked down, I realized that something was very, very wrong. . . .

MY COMPUTER WAS GONE!

As soon as I got over the **SHOCK**, I squeaked at the top of my lungs, "**Help!** Thief! Emergency! My computer is gone!"

Then I **FAINTED**.

I woke up with a start when Priscilla threw a bucket of **ice-cold** water on me. Brrr!

"I'm sorry, Mr. Stilton, but I'm all out of cheese salts!" she apologized. "You faint an awful lot, you know. But don't **worry** about your computer, sir. **TIP TOP TECH**, the computer company, **TOOK** it. You were sleeping so soundly when they arrived that I didn't want to wake you!"

I shook my snout and tried to clear my head. "I don't remember calling a computer company. My computer was **working just fine**!"

She frowned. "But, Mr. Stilton, they said that you asked to have the computer **fixed** in two shakes of a mouse's tail."

"I didn't call anyone!" I cried. There was something **STRANGE** about this — very **STRANGE**.

I had to focus on getting my computer back **AS SOON AS POSSIBLE**. That computer held the only copy of **THE GOLDEN BOOK**. There wasn't time to rewrite the whole thing!

I grabbed the phone and called Tip Top Tech. Right away, they put me on hold. Finally, a SCREECHY voice came on the line. "Good afternoon. This is TIP TOP TECH, the tip of the top in computer repair. My name is Shrilly McSqueaks. What can I do for you?"

"Good afternoon," I said, trying to keep my cool. "My name is Stilton, *Geronimo Stilton*. One of your technicians took my computer to be repaired, but there must be a MISTAKE. I never asked anyone to fix it."

I heard her typing for a minute. "Did you say your name was Stilton, *Geronimo Stilton*?"

"Yes, that's me." Were her ears filled with cheese?

"Are you sure?" she asked.

"**OF COURSE I'M SURE!**" I squeaked. "I should know own my name!"

"That's strange," she said. "I have a request here for a **SUPER-EXTRA-MEGA-URGENT** repair call from someone named Stilton, Geronimo Stilton, with your signature on it! Since I have you on the phone, can we talk about payment? For **SUPER-EXTRA-MEGA** repair calls, there's a **SUPER-EXTRA-MEGA** charge."

RANCID RICOTTA! My eyes bugged out of my head.

"In fact, we need your credit card number right now!" she continued. "Of course, if you don't want to pay now, you may pay in SUPER-EXTRA-MEGA easy monthly payments."

I buried my snout in my paws. "Listen, there's a SUPER-EXTRA-MEGA mistake here. I want my computer back right now!"

"I'm sorry, but I can't help you. Your computer is already on its way."

"On its way to where?" I yelped.

Shrilly McSqueaks cleared her throat. "Sir, there's no need to yell! Your computer is being shipped to our specialized SUPER-EXTRA-MEGA repair center in Cheddarton."

I didn't have another second to waste. "Did you say Cheddarton? Thanks!"

Before Shrilly McSqueaks could blast my eardrums again with her SCREECHY voice, I hung up. If my computer couldn't come to ME, I'd go to IT!

I rushed out of the office, CRYING, "Priscilla,

call my family — everyone but Grandfather William! Tell them to meet me at the airport in half an hour. It's urgent! We need to **HUNT FOR THE GOLDEN BOOK**!"

Where are you going?

To hunt for The Golden Book!

I KNEW
THAT MOUSE!

I dashed outside and jumped into the first **TAXI** I could find.

"To the airport, please! I need to get there *IMMEDIATELY*!" I cried.

The driver was **COOL**, calm, and collected. He answered without turning around. "As you wish, sir."

He stepped on the gas. That taxi screeched into the street, **BURNING RUBBER**. Yikes!

Quickly!

I buckled my seat belt and held on for dear life. Quaking with fear, I yelped, "Careful! I'm in a hurry, but I'd like to get there in one piece!"

The driver **SPED UP** even more, and I got even paler.

"Believe me, Mr. Stilton, you'd better get to the airport sooner rather than later. . . ." he said, **SLAMMING** his paw on the gas pedal.

I turned as white as mozzarella!

But I couldn't help thinking that the driver's voice seemed strangely familiar. Where had I heard it before?

I peeked at his reflection in the rearview mirror, and saw that he was wearing dark **SUNGLASSES**. His face looked strangely familiar, too. Where had I **SEEN** him before?

I was too scared — and too queasy! — to think much about it.

When we finally reached the airport, the taxi came to a dead stop. *Screeeeech!*

The driver's hat and sunglasses fell right off his snout. And in the rearview mirror, I saw his **COOL** expression, his dark eyes, and the hint of a smile that curled his lower lip just the *tiniest* bit. . . .

I knew that mouse! It was my friend **Kornelius von Kickpaw**!

He turned in his seat and grinned at me. "Here, these are special passes for **VIRs** — Very Important Rodents! They'll help you skip all the lines in the airport. There's a Tip Top Tech cargo plane at Gate Four that's about to *TAKE OFF* with your computer! If you hurry, you may be able to get it back before the plane *LEAVES*."

I was speechless. "Thank you, dear friend!"

He winked. "I've got your back, Geronimo. I know that you're always getting into **trouble**!"

Embarrassed, I twirled my whiskers. "You're right. But this time, it's all a big **MISUNDERSTANDING**!" I sighed. "A repairmouse took my computer by mistake! It holds the only copy of THE GOLDEN BOOK, and I don't have time to rewrite it."

Kornelius von Kickpaw raised his right eyebrow, tapped my forehead with his paw, and said, "USE YOUR HEAD, Geronimo. This was no mistake! Someone took your computer on purpose."

Double twisted rat tails! "But why?" I asked.

He tapped me on the forehead again. "USE YOUR HEAD! Think about who would get the most out of it, and then you'll know who took it!"

I was more confused than ever. I could really use a snack for inspiration — but there was no time. "Why take THE GOLDEN BOOK?" I wondered out loud. "It's only a story. . . ."

"I think you'll figure out the motive pretty soon," Kornelius said mysteriously. "Now HURRY— the Tip Top Tech plane is about to take off!"

Faster than LIGHTNING, I ran into the airport. Benjamin, Trap, and Thea were all waiting for me. I handed them each a VIR pass, and we dashed for the gate.

Trap wove between rushing rodents and wandering families, **HOWLING**, "Move! Look out! Mice coming through!"

Purple with embarrassment, I followed him, mumbling, "Uh . . . excuse me . . . pardon me . . . I'm so sorry . . . IT'S AN EMERGENCY!"

We finally made it to the gate — but it was too late.

The Tip Top Tech plane was already on the runway!

URGENT PACKAGE FOR TIP TOP TECH!

I ran up to the gate, screaming. "STOP, WAIT FOR ME! WE HAVE TO GET ON! My computer with *The Golden Book* is on boooooard!" But then an ENORMOUSE rodent picked me up by the tail and lifted me off the ground.

"Hey, you!" he boomed. "Where do you think you're going? Don't you see that this plane is about to *TAKE OFF*? Besides, that's a Tip Top Tech **cargo** plane — it's not carrying passengers. Do you want to sit with the boxes?"

"Well, ACTUALLY… yes!" I cried. This mouse was my last chance! "Please, I beg you. Take pity on a poor, *DESPERATE* rodent!"

But he wasn't convinced. In fact, he shook me

a few more times to get his message across . . . until Thea looked at him with her **VIOLET EYES**, and flashed him one of her most charming smiles.

Then she said sadly, "Don't beg, Geronimo. This rodent is only doing his job." She turned to the security mouse. "Sir, anyone can see

that you're a SPECIAL mouse. You won't hear another squeak from us!"

With a DRAMATIC sigh, Thea turned her head, pulled out a handkerchief, and dried a little fake *tEAR*.

What an ACTRESS!

Once he saw that she was crying, the security mouse IMMEDIATELY changed his mind. He dropped me with a THUMP (I think I bruised my tail!) and *RAN* after my sister, shouting, "Please don't cry, miss! You want to get on this *plane*, miss?"

Thea nodded, still pretending to dry her tears.

The security mouse boomed, "If you want to get on that plane, I'll help you. I'll do whatever it takes!"

Thea turned and said sweetly, "Oh, thank you. Do you think my family could join me? It's an **EMERGENCY**!"

The security mouse narrowed his eyes and pointed at me. "Everybody? Are you sure? How about this **CHEESEBRAIN** here?"

Offended, I cried, "I am not a **CHEESEBRAIN**! Though I do like to eat cheese . . . My name is Stilton, *Geronimo Stilton*! I'm an author, and I run *The Rodent's Gazette*!"

The security mouse *grabbed* his walkie-talkie and called the airplane pilot.

You're so kind!

Happy to help!

"Stop the engines!" he cried. "There's an URGENT PACKAGE for Tip Top Tech that needs to be loaded on board!"

"A PACKAGE? WHAT PACKAGE?" I whispered to Trap. He shrugged.

As the security mouse hurried off, promising to be right back, I asked Thea, "How did you do it? He doesn't look anything like the **BOSSY** rodent that grabbed me by the tail two minutes ago. . . ."

She winked. "In every rodent, there's a hidden gentlemouse. You just have to know how to find it!"

A few seconds later, the security mouse returned, carrying a **giant** box. He ushered us out onto the runway and hollered, "*HURRY UP* — all of you over here. Except you, miss!" He turned to Thea with a smile. "You'll be seated in the cockpit, next to the pilot!"

I suddenly **UNDERSTOOD** his plan. Holey cheese — we were going to fly in the cargo compartment of the plane. We were the **URGENT PACKAGE** for Tip Top Tech!

Without a second to waste, Trap, Benjamin, and I all **hid** behind the box.

The security mouse **LIFTED** the box and us with a **SPECIAL TRUCK**, placed us

You'll sit with the pilot!

Thank you!

in the plane's **cargo** compartment, and shouted, "Urgent package! Urgent package! Urrrrrrrrrrrgent package for TIP TOP TECH!"

I was shaking like a wobbly cheesecake, so I peeked out of the plane and asked him, "Isn't this a little *risky*? Will there be seat belts? I'm too fond of my fur! Are there any windows? I'm a little **CLAUSTROPHOBIC**. Do you have

any airsickness bags? I get **TERRIBLY** airsick. . . ."

The security mouse frowned and said, "Sorry, sir. **No** seat belts, **no** windows, **no** airsickness bags. You'll have to do the best you can! Use your IMAGINATION — after all, the famous Geronimo Stilton should have plenty of it." He waved. "Just be careful not to **get sick** on the boxes. There's valuable merchandise inside!"

Glub!

With that, the security mouse shut the hatch. The engines began to **RUMBLE**, and the plane zoomed down the runway. In two shakes of a mouse's tail, it had left the ground and was BOUNCING through the air.

Before we could find anything to grab on to,

we were **tossed** around and squished on top of one another. *Squeak!* What a massive 𝕄𝕆𝕌𝕊𝔼ℙ𝕀𝕃𝔼! The plane went UP AND DOWN.

UP AND DOWN.

UP AND DOWN.

Trap smushed my tail, his left paw was jammed inside my ear, and his elbow was **stuck** inside my snout.

As soon as I untangled

myself, I peered around and got a horrible **surprise**. The cargo hold was filled to the brim with big boxes — and they were all packed with computers that looked *just like mine*!

No! How would I ever find mine?

Noooo! How would I ever find mine?

Noooooooooooo!

THE HUNT FOR
THE GOLDEN BOOK!

Feeling hopeless, I began to squeak, "How am I going to find my computer? Where is *The Golden Book*? Wheeeeeeeere?"

Benjamin squeezed my paw. "Uncle Geronimo, is there anything **DIFFERENT** about your computer that could help you recognize it?" he asked.

I thought and thought and thought . . . until I finally remembered something! Thundering cat tails — I had probably **DENTED** my computer a few hours earlier, when I'd fallen asleep and given myself the enormouse LUMP on my forehead.

I squeaked happily, "Good thinking, Benjamin! Now I know exactly how to recognize my computer! Let's **HUNT FOR THE GOLDEN BOOK**!"

Benjamin and Trap brought me stack after stack of computers, and I checked them all one by one. I examined SEVEN THOUSAND THREE HUNDRED TWENTY-FIVE computers. My eyes were ready to fall out of my face! But finally, the SEVEN THOUSAND THREE HUNDRED TWENTY-SIXTH computer had a dent — right in the middle.

It fits!

I checked closely. The **BUMP** on my head fit perfectly into the dent. This was my computer! **FINALLY!**

I hugged it and whispered, **"MY little COMPUTeR!** No one will ever separate us again! I'll always keep you safe. . . ."

Trap **PINCHED** my ear.

"Great idea, Cuz! In fact, why don't you get a **CHAIN** so you can tie the computer to one of your paws at all times? Then you won't even have to **LOOK** for it again!" He winked.

Thrilled, I shouted, "What a **FaBUMOUSe iDea**, Trap! I'll get an elegant little silver chain — or how about a **HUGE**, titanium, anti-theft, anti-snatching, anti-cutting, anti-grabbing . . . anti-*everything* chain!"

I was studying my $\boxed{C}\boxed{O}\boxed{M}\boxed{P}\boxed{U}\boxed{T}\boxed{E}\boxed{R}$ to see how I could attach an anti-everything chain when I saw the **note** taped to the bottom. It was the **SUPER-EXTRA-MEGA-URGENT** repair order that Shrilly McSqueaks had told me about on the phone.

It was signed "Geronimo Stilton." But . . . that signature was a **FAKE**! I had never seen that order before in my life!

I noticed that the note gave off a nauseating scent, so strong and stinky it would have **knocked out** an elephant. I recognized it immediately: It was *Mademoiselle Manchego No. 8*, the perfume Sally Ratmousen has made especially for her by a company in Swissville.

SALLY RATMOUSEN!

She must have forged my signature and had my computer hauled away!

My whiskers trembled with **rage** and I shouted, "Sally, this time you went too far! Why did you do this? **Why?!**"

Just then, Thea opened the door and **ENTERED** the cargo hold.

"I'll tell you why, little brother! Sally doesn't want you to publish **THE GOLDEN BOOK** because it highlights the success of *The Rodent's*

Gazette! She's a very **Jealous** mouse."

I sighed and looked down at my paws. "Sally doesn't know that Grandfather William made so many corrections that now *The Golden Book* just talks about *him* and **ONLY** him!"

Hearing Grandfather William's name, Thea squeaked, "Cheesy creampuffs, Geronimo! We have to get the book to SUPER Print right away. Otherwise, it won't get **printed** in time, and Grandfather will be angrier than a cat in a cage!"

Whiskers whirling, I looked at my watch. "You're right — if we don't get it to SUPER Print in the next hour, it'll be too late!" I paced back and forth. "And if we don't publish the book, Grandfather won't win Lola's heart." I buried my face in my paws.

Thea said firmly, "I'LL TAKE CARE OF IT!"

She went back up to the cockpit. Before long,

she returned with a strange little backpack full of straps and buckles and said, "Put this on, Geronimo. And keep your computer **very close** to your chest. Understand?"

"**HUH?** What is that for?" I asked her.

Thea held up the backpack and helped me put my arms through the shoulder straps. "I'll tell you later, Geronimo. In the meantime, fasten the straps **TIGHT** and take one step **THAT WAY**. Okay, now another one, and another . . .

perfect!"

Then I saw her **WINK** at Trap. An instant later, she opened the door — and Trap **SHOVED** me out of the plane!

"Pull the cord, Geronimo!" Thea cried as I fell.

"Cord? What cord?"

For five fur-raising seconds

I was free-falling **DOWN**, **DOWN**, **DOWN** as the icy air whipped in my ears. Have I mentioned that I'm AFRAID of heights?

But just when I pictured myself splattering on the ground like a spilled mozzarella milkshake, I suddenly understood! I held on **TIGHT** to my computer with one trembling paw and yanked on the RIP CORD with the other. The parachute opened with a jerk. Whew!

READY FOR SHIPPING!

As I swung from the parachute and tried to ignore my churning stomach, I realized I was right above the **SUPER Print** building in Mouseport! Somehow, I landed on the building's roof, where a rodent dressed like a **SPRINTER** was waiting for me.

As soon as I landed, he asked, "Are you Mr. Stilton? Did you bring us 𝕿𝕳𝕰 𝕲𝕺𝕷𝕯𝕰𝕹 𝕭𝕺𝕺𝕶, the one that needs to be printed by tomorrow?"

"Yes, but the `layout` isn't quite right yet. . . ." I answered, out of breath. After all, I'd just **parachuted** out of a plane! What did a mouse have to do to catch a break around here?

He *SNATCHED* the computer from my paws and sprinted away, shouting, "There's no time to lose! We'll take care of everything! We'll **lay out** the book and print it immediately! Our motto is:

WE ARE SUPER-ULTRA-PRECISE AND EXTREMELY RAPID!"

While I figured out how to take off the parachute, the mouse *DASHED* to the printing room with my computer. I followed as fast as

I could, and saw that every rodent there wore **roller skates** to get around faster. Holey cheese! That's what I call **SPEEDY** service!

I was so busy watching all the mice zipping back and forth that I accidentally tripped a rodent in roller skates who was carrying an ENORMOUSLY HIGH pile of freshly printed books. The books all tumbled to the ground. Oops!

Red with EMBARRASSMENT, I bent over to help pick them up, MURMURING an

apology. Right then, another rodent in **roller skates** ran over my tail. Youch! He spun out of control and created a multiple-mouse pileup!

While everybody tumbled in a tangle of tails, roller skates, and books, I was thrown into the air. I landed on a **CONVEYOR BELT** carrying copies of *The Golden Book* fresh from the printer. But before I could even **admire** the books, my tie got caught . . . and I was suddenly packaged right along with them!

I shouted, "**Help!** Somebody unpack me!"
A rodent with **HUGE SCISSORS** quickly came to the rescue, but the owner of SUPER Print rushed over and cried, "Wait! Leave him! This way, he won't get into any more trouble." He pointed to the printing room door. "Why don't you load him into the van and **SHIP** him directly to New Mouse City with his books? And don't forget his $\boxed{C}\boxed{O}\boxed{M}\boxed{P}\boxed{U}\boxed{T}\boxed{E}\boxed{R}$. If he has to come back for it, he might cause even **more** of a mess!"

Up you go!

Two **MUSCLEMICE** loaded me into a van full of books. They even put a tag on me!

RECIPIENT:
THE RODENT'S GAZETTE
17 SWISS CHEESE CENTER
NEW MOUSE CITY 13131

ATTENTION: GERONIMO STILTON
WILLIAM SHORTPAWS

PS: DEAR MR. SHORTPAWS, IF YOU UNPACK THIS, WE CAN'T TAKE ANY RESPONSIBILITY FOR WHATEVER TROUBLE IT MAY CAUSE!

After a very long and bumpy trip (moldy Brie, I felt QUEASY!), I was finally unloaded at The Rodent's Gazette.

PINK, PINK, PINK . . . EVERYWHERE!

I arrived to find Grandfather William *gelled,* *slicked,* and *decked out* in a fancy pinstriped suit and patent leather shoes. *The Rodent's Gazette* meeting room had been transformed into a garden of pink *ROSES*, pink **STREAMERS**, little pink paper **Hearts**, and an enormouse ten-layer **CAKE** (pink, of course!). It was all in honor of Lola, who — you guessed it — adored pink!

As soon as Grandfather **unpacked** me, I said, "Don't you think you went a little overboard? This doesn't even look like *The Rodent's Gazette* office! It looks more like the headquarters for the **LONELY HEARTS CLUB**!"

Grandfather bellowed, "Geronimo, how can you complain? How UNGRATEFUL! I worked my tail off to organize all this, while you wasted time roaming around an airplane and parachuting *for fun*!"

I tried to tell him that I didn't have any fun at all, and that it was all Sally Ratmousen's **FAULT** that my computer was stolen with the only copy of THE GOLDEN BOOK on it. But Grandfather didn't give me time to squeak another word before he stuck an **invoice** under my nose. It must have been at least ten paws long!

"This is the list of trouble you caused at **SUPER Print**. It's only because of Frank Fastmouse and his fast talking that the printer didn't sue us for **damages**!"

Frank Fastmouse looked up from where he stood nearby and said, "You caused quite a MESS, Mr. Stilton!"

Everyone shook their heads, murmuring, "Oh, Geronimo, you're always so clumsy!"

I couldn't help feeling **S A D**. Was that really what they all thought of me?

I slunk away, muttering, "Since I'm not welcome here, I'm leaving! I won't trouble you anymore! I need to ReST because, even though no one seems to care, it's been days and days and days since I've slept. I was too busy writing **THE GOLDEN BOOK**!"

I was as glum as a mouse with no cheese.

This was supposed to be a party celebrating **TEN YEARS** of writing and publishing my books. Instead, everyone was **ganging up** on me! It just didn't seem fair.

As I left the room, I walked by the cake that Grandfather William had ordered. It was an amazing tower of pink **frosting**, pink candy

HeaRTS, and pink sugar *ROSES*. I noticed that a little drop of (pink!) mascarpone cheese cream had dripped on the tray. I couldn't resist — I scooped it up with my paw. It looked so **DELICIOUS**!

I closed my eyes and took a taste . . . but suddenly my mouth was on **fire**! My whiskers stood on end. The cake was **SaLty** — and spicy! Someone had substituted salt instead of sugar, and had added lots of **HOT CHILI POWDER**.

Yuck!

Who would have done such a thing?

Before I could figure it out, something odd happened. I heard a **BUZZ** . . . then a **CLICK** . . . then a **BEEEEEEEP**. Suddenly, I saw a thin wisp of **GREEN SMOKE**, and a horrendous

stink came from the pink roses all over the room!

Everyone ran outside, **paler** than mozzarella, holding our snouts and **shouting**, "What a terrible smell!"

I had just taken a deep breath of fresh air when my cell phone rang. Uh-oh — it was **SALLY RATMOUSEN**!

"Geronimo, how's the preparation for your **PARTY** going?"

I answered, "There won't be any party, Sally. Someone has **sabotaged** it! And I think I know who: the same rodent who tried to prevent me from publishing **THE GOLDEN BOOK** by making my computer disappear. . . ."

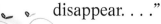

Sally scoffed. "How dare you, Stilton! Are you trying to SUGGEST that I put chili powder in the cake and stunk up the flowers?"

I knew it! "Aha! It *was* you! How else would you know about the chili powder and the stinky flowers? I never told you *why* the party was ruined!"

There was a pause before Sally squeaked, "Oh, I don't care if you FIGURED me out!" She chuckled. "Good luck with your little party!"

CLICK!

WE'RE STRONG —
VERY STRONG!

Dejected, I headed home. I had to call and tell everyone that the party was canceled.

IT WAS ALL FOR NOTHING.

All those hours spent writing . . . the big lump on my head . . . the terrifying adventure to track

down my computer and THE GOLDEN BOOK . . . all for nothing!

But when I got home, there was a SURPRISE waiting for me: Kornelius von Kickpaw and Frank Fastmouse.

As soon as Kornelius

saw me he said, "I hope you're not planning to **give up**, Geronimo!"

"Remember, Geronimo," Frank added, "I'm just one mouse, and you're just one mouse, but if we all work together . . ."

". . . *we are strong — very strong!*" I finished, with a smile on my snout. "With your help, maybe we can still pull this party off!"

Frank called his GOOD friend Frederick Fuzzypaws, the mayor of New Mouse City, and asked his permission to use New Mouse City's **MAIN SQUARE** for the party. I called everyone I could think of, explained what had HAPPENED, and told them, "Let's meet in Singing Stone Plaza at nine tonight! Tell all your friends to bring a **CAKE** and a birthday candle. Spread the word!"

While I was busy doing that, Kornelius CALLED Thea, Trap, Benjamin, and all my other relatives

and friends and asked each of them to pitch in.

Aunt Sweetfur promised to make ten **giant** pots of chocolate cheese pudding (my favorite!). Thea offered to take care of the **decorations**. Benjamin and his friends put together a **BAND** to liven up the party, and Trap took care of the *LIGHTING*.

By nine o'clock, everything was ready. Singing Stone Plaza looked **amazing**, and every rodent in the city was there. I could hardly believe it, but we'd done it!

IT WAS A FABUMOUSE PARTY!

That's because we'd all worked together. And many mice brought a **CAKE** with a birthday candle right in the middle. Yum — that was a lot of cake!

When the time came to blow out the candles, we all blew them out together. This **PARTY** wasn't just to celebrate my **books** anymore.

This party was for everyone!

As for Grandfather and Lola . . .

They danced the entire night away under the stars.

I danced the night away, too — with Petunia Pretty Paws, the rodent of my dreams!

When the party ended at dawn, I went to track down my grandfather. I wanted to find

Petunia!

Awesome!

out if he had told Lola how he felt, and if she'd finally reciprocated his *love*. I hoped he had been **BRAVER** than me! (As usual, I still hadn't found the courage to share my **FeeLINGS** with Petunia Pretty Paws. I'm such a 'fraidy mouse!)

I couldn't find grandfather anywhere, but when I got home I found a note from him.

Dear Grandson,

I know I have always told you that work is the most important thing in life, but tonight I learned an important lesson. Love is the only thing that can truly give our lives meaning! That's why I'm leaving tonight to take Lola on a long, romantic cruise around the world. And when we come back, who knows — maybe we'll get married!

Take care of <u>The Rodent's Gazette</u> while I'm away. I know it's in good hands because, even if I've never told you, I'm proud of you, and I love you!

Grandfather William

I couldn't believe my eyes! It seemed **impossible** that my grandfather had written this note. After all, rodents didn't call him Cheap Mouse Willie for nothing! But *love* — true love — can really change a mouse for the **BETTER**.

And now that Grandfather William had found love, the whole fur-raising hunt for **THE GOLDEN BOOK** was really, truly worth it!

As I sat down in my chair, I started thinking about what to WRITE next. . . . I couldn't wait to see what my **NEXT TEN YEARS** of adventures would be!

Now check out this bonus
Mini Mystery story!
Join me in solving a whisker-licking-
good mystery. Find clues along with me
as you read. Together, we'll be
super-squeaky investigators!

Geronimo Stilton

THE LAKE
MONSTER

TURN ON YOUR TV RIGHT AWAY!

It was a warm spring morning. I was feeding my dear little fishy, Hannibal, when — Oh, pardon me, I almost forgot to introduce myself! My name is Stilton, *Geronimo Stilton*. I run *The Rodent's Gazette*, the most famouse newspaper on Mouse Island.

Now, where was I? Oh, yes, I was feeding Hannibal when the phone *rang*. I was so startled I accidentally dumped *too much* food into his tank.

"Geronimo, it's Thea. Turn on your TV right away! I'll call you back in a minute!" It was my sister, Thea. **What could possibly be so urgent?**

I had just hung up the phone when it *rang* again. As soon as I answered, I heard a *shout* so loud it made me knock half the fish food onto the floor.

"Grandson, it's me! Turn on your

TV **IMMEDIATELY**! Go on now, move those paws! I'll call you back in a minute!" It was my grandfather William Shortpaws, founder of *The Rodent's Gazette*. **What could possibly be so urgent?**

I was heading toward my TV when the phone rang again. I was so surprised I **JUMPED** into the air, and a good bit of fish food fell into my open snout.

"Hi, G! Are you **WATCHING** TV?"

"Blugh . . . phug . . . ptui . . . ptui . . . ," I responded, **spitting** out the fish food.

"What?!" she said. "Turn on your

TV right away! I'll call you back in a minute."

It was **Petunia Pretty Paws**! She is the most fascinating mouse I know. She's a TV journalist who has dedicated her life to defending the environment. **But what could possibly be so urgent?**

I had just picked up the remote control when the doorbell *rang*.

I tripped on the carpet, and the rest of the fish food went **flying** . . . everywhere!

Hannibal

BREAKING NEWS!

I opened my front door and was immediately run over by two tiny CYCLONES!

"Hurry, Uncle Geronimo, turn on your TV!" they exclaimed.

It took me a moment to recover from my surprise. By then, my adorable nephew BENJAMIN and his friend Bugsy Wugsy, Petunia Pretty Paws's niece, were curled up on my couch.

"Hello, my little cheese niblets," I said affectionately. "Would one of you mind telling me wha —"

"Ssshh!" **hissed** Bugsy Wugsy.

I turned my attention to the TV screen. A newscaster was interviewing **Sally Ratmousen**, my number one enemy!

"When did you see the **MONSTER** for the first time?" the newscaster asked.

"As I said, a friend of mine who lives on the lake saw it yesterday, and he called

Come on, Uncle! Hurry up!

me **AT ONCE** to tell me about it!"

"Could you tell us what it looks like?" the newscaster asked.

"Listen, if you want to know that, I suggest you go buy the **special edition** of my newspaper, *The Daily Rat.* Right now! At once! Immediately!"

"Do you have **PHOTOS** of it?"

"Of course! There is a huge picture of the **LAKE MONSTER** on the front page!"

Oh, for the love of cheese! Had I heard correctly? A lake monster? And *The Daily Rat,* our rival newspaper, was coming out with a **special edition** about it? I had a feeling I'd be hearing from Grandfather William about this.

THERE'S NOT A MOMENT TO LOSE!

A split second later, the telephone began to **ring**. As I'd suspected, the first to call me back was Grandfather William. He was shouting even more

I hate to travel. . . .

loudly than before. "Hello, Grandson? Did you hear? You need to leave for the lake right away! Move it! **THERE'S NOT A MOMENT TO LOSE!**"

"But, Grandfather, you know I hate to travel. . . ."

It was too late to protest. He'd already hung up.

Next Thea called me back. "Gerry Berry, did you hear the news? We need to leave right away! THERE'S NOT A MOMENT TO LOSE! I'll be right over."

"But, Thea, you know I hate to travel. . . ."

It was too late to protest. She'd already hung up.

Petunia Pretty Paws was the last to call. "Hi, G! Did you hear? We can't miss out on a chance like this! It could be a rare animal we thought was extinct!

We need to leave right away. **THERE'S NOT A MOMENT TO LOSE!** I'll be right over."

This time, I didn't even try to protest. I hate to travel, but I would do anything for Petunia!

I was lost in a daydream about a **romantic** canoe ride with Petunia when I felt someone tugging at my JACKET. It was Benjamin and Bugsy.

"Uncle Geronimo, can we come, too?" asked Benjamin.

"I don't know, Benjamin," I said. "It could be DANGEROUS. . . ."

"Come on, Uncle G!" Bugsy pleaded. "Nothing bad will happen as long as you're there to protect us."

Their furry little faces were so hopeful I just couldn't let them down. So I **hugged** Benjamin and Bugsy and said, "Oh, all right. We'll go find the LAKE MONSTER together!"

LEAVING FOR THE LAKE

We decided it would be best to
TRAVEL together in Petunia's car.
Since I am a true gentlemouse, I let Thea
sit in the front seat, while
I climbed in BACK with
Bugsy, BENJAMIN, and
all our baggage.

"Are you comfy,
Geronimo?"
asked Petunia,
looking in her
rearview mirror.
"Mpffh . . .

fllbb!" I responded. My snout was full of the **synthetic cat fur** on Thea's suitcase.

Petunia gave me a funny smile. "You know, G, you're squeaking very strangely today."

"That's because my brother is a **very strange** mouse," Thea declared. "Don't tell me you've never noticed."

Petunia and Thea took turns driving. They spent the whole ride *chatting*, while Benjamin and Bugsy passed the time playing Rat, Paper, Scissors.

Petunia stopped three times to let us stretch our **paws**. For me, that turned out to be three times too many!

At the **first stop**, I had to unload and reload all the luggage to get Petunia's notebook from the very bottom bag.

At the **second stop**, I had to change a flat tire all by myself while Petunia and Thea just stood there yammering away.

At the **third stop**, everything went smoothly . . . until we tried to leave, that is. We ran out of gas, and I had to push the car the rest of the way!

But for Petunia, I would have climbed CHEDDAR CRAG with one paw tied behind my tail. And without complaining, either!

At the Golden Catfish

At the lake, there was a nasty surprise waiting for us: Every TELEVISION STATION and newspaper on Mouse Island had sent REPORTERS and **photographers**! Plus, many curious rodents were visiting. There were mice everywhere, and everyone was talking about the LAKE MONSTER.

We made our way to the only hotel in the area, THE GOLDEN CATFISH, where the rooms were going like hot cheese buns. Fortunately, Thea had reserved five beds ahead of time.

Islet

Castle ruins

The hotel's **manager**, followed by two rodents who were as thin as string cheese, came to meet us.

"Good evening, *heh heh heh*! My name is **SAMUEL SWEETWATER**, and I am the manager of the Golden Catfish.

Welcome! Did you have a nice trip?"

"Yes, it was fabumouse!" my friends responded. I couldn't squeak a word since I was still trying to catch my breath after pushing the car.

"Is this gentlemouse with you?" Sweetwater asked, pointing to me.

"Yes, of course . . . *pant* . . . ," I responded. "My name is . . . *pant* . . . Stilton, *Geronimo Stilton* . . . *pant . . . pant . . .*"

"Geronimo Stilton? The famouse writer? It is a real HONOR to have you here with us!" he said, shaking my paw vigorously. "This place really needs a bit of **publicity**, *heh heh heh*! I was

very lucky to be down by the lake *LAST WEEK* when the monst —"

"Last week!" I exclaimed. "But on the news they said that the **MONSTER** was first seen yesterday."

Sweetwater stammered, "Um — yes, that is — I meant to say — last **NIGHT**."

"And you were the one to contact Ms. Ratmousen?" I asked, finally able to free myself from his PAWSHAKE.

"Yes," he replied. "Sally — I mean, Ms. Ratmousen — is an old acquaintance of mine. When she heard the NEWS, she wanted to buy the exclusive rights to the story. She pays very well, you know."

"My newspaper pays very well, too," I said.

"Of course, *heh heh heh*!" Sweetwater sneered. "But you see, Mr. Stilton, I've known Sally — I mean, Ms. Ratmousen — for so many years that I immediately thought of her."

He was still squeaking when my cell phone rang. Grandfather William thundered, "Grandson, are you at the lake yet? **MOVE THAT TAIL!**"

"Yes, Grandfather, I —"

"It's about time! I've sent up a photographer. He's there, waiting for you. **SO MOVE THOSE PAWS!**"

"But, Grandfather, I —"

"No thanks necessary, Grandson!

You can show your gratitude by getting busy out there! I want **PICTURES** of this monster by **TOMORROW** night! **SO MOVE IT!**"

"Grandfather, can you listen for a —?"

But he had already hung up. Rats!

"If you follow me, I'll show you to your rooms, *heh heh heh*!" **SAMUEL SWEETWATER** said. He turned to the two thin **rodents**. "**ZIP! ZAP!** Take these bags inside."

CLUE1

What did Samuel Sweetwater say about the monster that seemed a bit strange?

AN ATTIC FIT FOR A KING

As we headed to our rooms, Mr. Sweetwater turned to squeak with us. "Unfortunately, I only have one four-rodent room left. For the fifth, I thought of a **simple but comfortable** solution.

Like the gentlemouse I am, I accepted the "simple but comfortable" solution.

"Follow me to the **ATTIC**, Mr. Stilton."

"The *attic*?" I asked, lugging my bag up the **STAIRS**. Why, oh, why hadn't I stayed home?

"The bathroom is on the first floor, only **ten flights of stairs** down. For an athletic rodent like yourself, I'm sure it will be nothing, *heh*! Naturally, the **H⊙T** water will cost you just a little bit extra. . . ."

Why, oh, why hadn't I stayed home?

"Is the bed **soft**?" I asked.

"The mattress is ⓝⓐⓣⓤⓡⓐⓛ ⓢⓣⓡⓐⓦ!

Just be careful of the holes in the roof — some BATS might come in. . . ."

Bats?!? Why, oh, why hadn't I stayed home?

Samuel Sweetwater threw open the door to the attic. "You and your roommate will do just fine here!"

As I stepped in, a powerful FLASH blinded me!

"My name is Stevie Snapson, and I never botch my shot!" my new roommate declared.

This had to be the photographer that Grandfather William had sent.

SALLY'S PHOTOGRAPHER

When I went down for dinner, more **unpleasant** surprises awaited me.

SALLY RATMOUSEN was seated at the table next to ours. As soon as she saw me, she attacked. "Stilton! What in the name of cheddar are **you** doing here?"

"I'm here to photograph the **LAKE MONSTER**, Sally," I responded.

"You're a little **LATE**, old friend.

This time, I've got the scoop. **LOOK!**" She shoved a photo of the monster **UNDER** my snout. It was

hard to see it too clearly because of the fog, but it really was quite striking.

"Let me introduce you to the author of this masterpiece," Sally declared. "This is Ricky Zoomson, my best photographer."

A scrawny rodent poked out from behind her. He shot me a **smirk**.

Trying to remain calm, I responded,

"Well, Sally, you've made the first move, but the next PHOTO will be ours. You can bet on it!"

Ricky Zoomson

"I don't think so! Anyway, the **MONSTER** won't show his snout until tomorrow at **dawn**," Sally replied.

"How do you know that?" I demanded.

But she had already STOMPED away. This situation was getting **stranger** by the second!

I sat down at our table, but I couldn't take my EYES off that photo of the monster. The more I looked at it, the more convinced I became that something wasn't right.

As soon as Petunia saw the photo, she **exclaimed**, "What an unusual-looking monster! There's definitely something **fishy** about it. . . ."

That worried me. "Do you think it could be **dangerous**?"

"Don't go all 'fraidy mouse on me!" exclaimed Thea. "We'll think about the **MONSTER** tomorrow. Let's get some shut-eye!"

CLUE 2

Before Sally left, what did she say that was strange?

A BATHROOM, QUIIIIICK!

It wasn't a very peaceful night for me, dear reader. Stevie Snapson snored louder than my uncle Nibbles when he has a cold. Plus, anytime I managed to nod off for more than a few minutes, I dreamed of the **MONSTER**.

Suddenly, I had a *very urgent* need . . . to go to the bathroom!

I raced down ten flights of stairs, but tripped over the last step . . .

I raced down the **ten** flights of stairs that separated me from the first floor, but I tripped over the last **step** and landed in front of the hotel entrance.

Just when I thought there was no way I was going to make it, I saw a yellow arrow pointing to the bathroom.

I scurried in as quickly as I could!

That's when I heard some squeaking from the next room.

"Why do we need to wear oxygen

. . . and landed on my tail in front of the hotel entrance!

masks?" said a voice.

"Because this time the **MONSTER** will stay underwater. Only the head will appear. We can't let anyone see the **broken** tail!"

"Let's go. Boss said not to be late!"

I snuck out to see who was *talking*, but I must have just missed them!

Who were they? How did they know so much about the monster? And who was their **boss**?

The door was open, so I peeked inside the room. I spotted wet suits, flippers, masks, and other underwater **GEAR**. Things were getting **stranger and stranger**!

AN ANONYMOUSE NOTE

I raced up to the attic and tried to wake Stevie. No luck! Now his **SNORING** was louder than a marching band.

I sighed. I was tired, too. I tried putting my **pillow** over my head, but I could still hear him.

I turned this way and that, curling my tail around my ears to try to block out the sound. But I just couldn't sleep. I was lying there with my **eyes** wide open when I noticed something.

Someone had SLIPPED an envelope UNDER the door. But who?

My whiskers were shivering with suspense. I quickly opened the *envelope* and scanned the note inside.

IF YOU BELIEVE IN THE MONSTER WHO LIVES IN THE LAKE, COME DOWN TO THE SHORE BEFORE DAWN BREAKS, IN FRONT OF THE CASTLE RUINS, YOU WILL GET TO SEE THE MONSTER – IN ALL OF HIS BEAUTY!

SIGNED,
A FRIEND OF YOURS

Something smelled **fishier** than day-old tuna. This **anonymouse** note told me so many details about the **MONSTER** appearing!

CLUE 3

Why does Geronimo think there's something suspicious about the note?

A BUMPY RIDE

SUDDENLY, Stevie woke up. Instantly, he was clicking his **FLASH** button. "Where's the monster? Take me to him!"

I showed him the note. We decided we couldn't miss this chance to see the monster **ourselves**.

Outside, it was **really foggy**. We ran into **MR. SWEETWATER** in front of the hotel. "Can I give you a paw, Mr. Stilton?" he asked.

"We need to get to the other side of the **lake**, but our car is out of gas," I explained to him.

"Can you drive a motorcycle?"

"**I can!**" said Stevie.

The hotel manager smirked. "Don't worry, Mr. Stilton, it will only cost you a little bit extra, *heh heh heh. . . .*"

A few minutes later, I was buckled into the SIDECAR of an ancient motorcycle

as it zoomed over the bumpy dirt road that circled the lake. Stevie was in the driver's seat.

When we arrived at the other side of the lake, in front of the castle ruins, Stevie tried to BRAKE — but ended up crashing into an oak tree!

WHAT A CAT-ASTROPHE!!!

The motorcycle was totaled, but we were okay, thank goodmouse! And we'd made it. We were the ONLY ONES there! Now we just had to hope that the MYSTERIOUS note told the truth.

Suddenly, the lake water began to bubble. We could see something dark moving under the surface. . . .

THE MONSTER'S TAIL

A long, thick tail suddenly burst through the water's surface!

"Hurry, Stevie!" I yelled. **"Shoot! Shoot!"**

At that moment, a dozen other flashes went off. A herd of photographers popped out of the BRUSH. Everyone RACED for the lake as if they had a pack of hungry cats on their tails. SALLY'S photographer Ricky Zoomson pushed me so hard I ended up IN THE WATER! The monster's twitching tail missed me by a WHISKER.

I thrashed and splashed my way back to shore. By then, the MONSTER had disappeared under the waves once more.

The author of the mysterious note had tricked me. He had given everyone the same information. THERE WENT MY EXCLUSIVE!

A STRANGE PHOTO

We returned to the hotel on paw. Mr. Sweetwater greeted us with his usual smarmy **smile**. "Mr. Stilton, how'd you do on the motorcycle? *Heh heh heh!*"

I turned **pinker** than a naked mole rat. "Well, you see . . . that is . . . we got into a bit of a **WRECK**. . . ."

"Oh, don't worry about it," Mr. Sweetwater jeered. "We'll get it fixed in the blink of a cat's eye. It'll just cost you *a little bit* extra, *heh heh heh*!"

We went up to our room. While Stevie developed the **ROLLS** of film, I collapsed on my straw mattress and tried to get some sleep.

An hour later, we headed downstairs for breakfast. Thea was there with Benjamin and Bugsy, who **hugged** me. Petunia bounced over to me as well. "This place is a marvemouse natural oasis! We absolutely must prevent

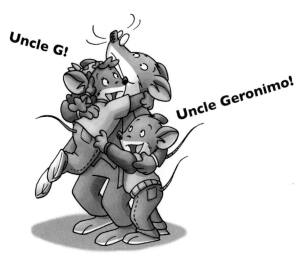

Uncle G!

Uncle Geronimo!

anyone from ruining it. Especially now that the news about the LAKE MONSTER is everywhere."

"Did you get a photo of the MONSTER?" Benjamin asked.

I showed them the

photos. "Yes! Well, sort of . . ."

"You can see the monster in this one!" exclaimed **Bugsy Wugsy**. Or at least part of him . . ."

Stevie and I took a **closer** look. "See — I never botch my shot!" he exclaimed triumphantly.

I **gazed** and **gazed** at the photo: Something about the monster's *tail* seemed odd. But what?

CLUE 4

What looks odd about the monster's tail?

THE RAT RACE

The next day, every newspaper on Mouse Island had a **HUGE** headline about the Lake Monster on its front page. And they all **PRINTED** better photos than ours!

When my cell phone rang, I knew right away who it would be: **Grandfather William**.

"What is this rubbish we published, Grandson?!" he screeched. "You better not be cramping Stevie's style!"

"No, Grandfather, it's just that —"

"**NO EXCUSES!** Tomorrow I want a photo that's good enough to fill the entire front page. Do you hear me? MOVE IT! GET THE PICTURE! GO!"

When I ran into Sally Ratmousen, she waved the second SPECIAL EDITION of *The Daily Rat* under my snout. "Watch and learn, Stilton, watch and learn! At *The Daily Rat*, we don't settle for a measly picture of a monster's tail! It's all or nothing, I say! This is a rat race, after all!"

When I looked at Sally's newspaper, I felt my heart sink all the way to my PAWS.

Suddenly, BENJAMIN exclaimed, "But this photo couldn't have been taken by Ricky Zoomson! Look where the castle ruins are. . . ."

We looked more closely at Sally's newspaper. BENJAMIN was right!

This whole story was starting to stink worse than rotten Gouda. It was time to uncover the truth!

CLUE 5

Why couldn't Ricky Zoomson have taken this photo with the other photographers?

THE SECOND ANONYMOUSE NOTE

That night was even worse than the one before. Stevie was **SNORING** loud enough to wake a comatose cat. I just couldn't sleep!

All at once, I had a brilliant idea: I could figure out whom I'd heard in the room near the bathroom.

I went **DOWN** to the first floor. As soon as I entered the bathroom, I heard squeaking from the room next door.

"What do you mean, we need to go back underwater?"

"Well, the tail wasn't supposed to be

visible yesterday! It was all because of that CLUMSY rodent who fell into the lake. This time, the MONSTER'S HEAD WILL RISE out of the water. . . ."

They were the same voices as before! And they were squeaking about me!

I peeked through the keyhole and saw two rodents dressed in scuba gear. Strange, very strange! I was sure I had seen those two before, but

couldn't remember where.

I crept out of the bathroom to follow them, but they had already disappeared.

Discouraged, I climbed back to the **ATTIC**. That was when I saw another *envelope* by the door.

> IF YOU WANT TO BEAT YOUR RIVAL,
>
> MAKE SUNRISE THE TIME OF YOUR ARRIVAL.
>
> TAKE HEART AND COME DOWN TO THE SWAMP
>
> IF YOU WANT TO SEE THE MONSTER ROMP!
>
> SIGNED,
> A FRIEND OF YOURS

MOUSEYBACK RIDE ON THE MONSTER

Just before sunup, Stevie and I again stood at the entrance to the GOLDEN CATFISH.

SAMUEL SWEETWATER was also there, and asked me his usual question: "Can I give you a paw with anything, Mr. Stilton? *Heh heh heh!*"

"Can you tell me how to reach the SWAMP?" I asked timidly.

Mr. Sweetwater smirked as he replied, "Oh, it's easy. Just follow that path for about a mile. A TANDEM bicycle might get you there quicker. It'll cost you . . ."

"I know, I know," I said, rolling my eyes. "Just a little bit extra!"

After Stevie and I had pedaled for

about five minutes, the bike began to **sink** into the mud. We had to continue through the muck by paw. Blech!

The fog was so thick we could hardly see our paws. Then suddenly, the monster's back emerged from the water!

"Quick, Stevie! **Shoot!**" I shouted.

"Where? Where? WHERE?" he cried, taking pictures at random.

"Over there, on the lake!"

Once again, other **photographers** poked their snouts out of the shrubs and headed straight for the MONSTER. And Ricky Zoomson pushed me into the water AGAIN!

I was flailing around, when suddenly

the monster came up from the depths —
and I found myself on its back!

"Stevie, TAKE THE PICTUUUURE!"
I screeched. I was scared out of my fur.

The last thing I saw was the flash
from his camera — at that moment, the
monster flung me toward shore!

"AAAHHHHH!"

WHAT HAPPENED?

When I woke up, I was back at the hotel.

"How are you feeling, Uncle Geronimo?" Benjamin asked.

"All right," I mumbled, opening my eyes. "What happened?"

"You RODE the Lake Monster," Benjamin said. "Look!" He showed me the front page of *The Rodent's Gazette* with MY picture front and center.

"You see?" Stevie said proudly. "I told you I never botch my shot!"

"You were very COURAGEOUS, G!" said Petunia, making me blush. She

is such a *fascinating mouse*!

My cell phone rang. As soon as I answered it, I heard Grandfather William's voice squawking: "Grandson, what a photo! Have you seen it? Snapson is **worth his weight in cheese**! I want more photos just like that, but clearer! Do you hear me? MOVE IT! SNAP THOSE PICS!"

TAKE A LOOK-SEE!

Well, Grandfather was happy, so at last I could relax! Thank goodmouse.

My relief didn't last long, since Sally Ratmousen soon burst into the room. "Stilton! **Congratulations!** You took a really nice photo!"

"Thank you, **Sally**," I responded with satisfaction. "As you can see, my **newspaper** is just as good as yours!"

"Oh, of course," she replied. "But my **photographer** is even better than yours. Didn't I tell you that I am always right? Take a look-see!" She shoved a

close-up photo of the **MONSTER'S FACE**
under my snout. "That monster is mine,
and I won't let you have him!"

With that, she left,

SLAMMING

the door behind her.

ANOTHER SLEEPLESS NIGHT

Stevie snored again that night. He was loud enough to wake a dead rat. As usual, I wasn't able to sleep a **wink**!

My mind was racing like a hamster on a wheel. I thought about the story of the monster, our attempts to photograph him, Sally's scoop, Mr. Sweetwater's strange behavior, and those two suspicious rodents in the room next to the bathroom. I was so confused. . . .

But I knew I needed to find those two rodents! I got out of bed, crept down the stairs, and headed into the bathroom.

It was then that my LUCK changed. From the room next door I could hear squeaks that I knew quite well by now. "But, Sally, that's too dangerous!"

"I don't care!" Sally replied. "Are you telling me that simpleton Stilton can climb on the monster and I can't?! I want to be in a picture sitting astride the monster! RIGHT NOW! AT ONCE!"

"Okay, Sally, we'll meet at the center of the lake at MIDNIGHT on the dot," said Mr. Sweetwater. "You two, go get ready."

"You better not be late, not even by a minute — or else! Now get out, you **cheeseheads**!"

Then I saw **SALLY** and Samuel Sweetwater leave the room, followed by the two scuba divers. At last, I'd figured out who they were!

I ran to wake up Thea, Petunia, Benjamin, Bugsy Wugsy, and Stevie. It was our turn to *JOIN THE ACTION*!

CLUE 6

Do you recognize the two scuba divers?

A Surprise from the Sky

An hour later, Stevie and I were in a life raft, smack-dab in the middle of the lake, waiting for the **MONSTER** to appear. It was a moonless **night**.

My tail was trembling with fright!

After a few minutes of silence, we heard the thrum of a **motorBoat**

approaching at top speed. Its lights were off, so the rodents on board couldn't see us. But we could hear their voices.

"Hurry up! I don't want to catch a cold out here on your chilly lake!"

"Stay calm, Sally — Zip and Zap will be here any moment. *Heh heh heh!*"

"They better be!" Sally snapped. "Now, Ricky, try to get the shot this time. I'm tired of having to retouch your **abominable** photos!"

Suddenly, we heard a rumbling in the distance. The monster was approaching from the bottom of the lake!

"Get ready to shoot, Stevie, but only when I say so!" I whispered.

"Snapson never botches his shot!"
he declared, standing up with his camera.

At that moment, a wave from
the monster made the raft rock, and
Stevie went snoutdown into the water!
He hit the FLASH button on his
way in, and the surface of the lake lit up.

Naturally, Sally noticed us. "Stilton!"
she yelled. "Don't you know when to

throw in the cheesecloth?"

I didn't answer — I was too busy trying to fish Stevie out of the lake!

Meanwhile, the **MONSTER** was getting closer. Just when it seemed like we were about to end up as his food, a HELICOPTER appeared above us. It was Thea and Petunia!

At last, I managed to pull Stevie back onto the raft, but by now the monster was practically on top of us!

That was when a ROPE ladder fell out of the helicopter and into my paws. Stevie and I grabbed it. We escaped the monster by a WHISKER!

THE BELLY OF THE BEAST

Incredibly, Stevie had managed to photograph the **MONSTER** underwater!

"See? Snapson never botches his shot! Never!" he boasted.

The next day, the photo was on the front page of *The Rodent's Gazette*. In the article that accompanied it, I explained what that **SCOUNDREL** Samuel Sweetwater had done.

The monster was a **FAKE**! Samuel Sweetwater had cooked up this monstrous **SCAM** to get more tourists to come to the lake. He hoped to expand his hotel and

make a small fortune.

And **SALLY**? Well, with the exclusive to the story, her newspaper would have **SOLD** millions of copies. But instead, it was *The Rodent's Gazette* that set a new sales record!

Samuel and Sally had to go to **court** to face fraud charges. A judge made them pay a **huge** fine. Thanks to a suggestion from Petunia, the money was used to help build a magnificent **natural park** at the lake. It became a wildlife preserve where rodents can play, hike, and go bike riding, **WITHOUT DANGER!**

Can you guess what the park's main **attraction** is? Riding around

the lake on the monster's back!
And guess who does all the pedaling to
power the monster: Samuel Sweetwater,
Zip, and Zap!

YOU'RE THE INVESTIGATOR!

DID YOU FIGURE OUT THE CLUES?

1 **What did Samuel Sweetwater say about the monster that seemed a bit strange?**

He said that he had seen it "last week," but Sally reported that the monster had first been seen just the day before.

2 **Before Sally left, what did she say that was strange?**

She said the monster would appear at dawn. How could she possibly know that?

3 **Why does Geronimo think there's something suspicious about the note?**

Because the author of the note knew where and when the monster would appear. How could he or she know that?

4 **What looks odd about the monster's tail?**

There's a bandage on the monster's tail! It's broken, just like the two rodents in the room next to the bathroom said.

5 **Why couldn't Ricky Zoomson have taken this photo with the other photographers?**

In the background you can see the castle ruins, but Ricky Zoomson was on the shore in front of the ruins. Therefore, this photo was taken at a different time and from a different spot on the lakeshore.

6 **Do you recognize the two scuba divers?**

They are Zip and Zap!

HOW MANY QUESTIONS DID YOU ANSWER CORRECTLY?

ALL 6 CORRECT: You are a SUPER-SQUEAKY INVESTIGATOR!

FROM 2 TO 5 CORRECT: You are a SUPER INVESTIGATOR! You'll get that added squeak soon!

LESS THAN 2 CORRECT: You are a GOOD INVESTIGATOR! Keep practicing to get super-squeaky!

Farewell until the next mystery!

Geronimo Stilton

Q **Why was the mouse carrying the ladder?**

A So he could get to high school!

Q **Where is the best place to put cheese?**

A In your belly!

Q **What did the blanket say to the mouse?**

A "Don't worry, I've got you covered!"

Q **Why did the mouse sit on the watch?**

A She wanted to be on time!

Q Why did the mouse take a ruler to bed?

A So he could measure how long he slept!

Q What time does a duck wake up?

A At the *quack* of dawn!

Q What do pigs need when they are hurt?

A *Oink*ment!

Q Have you heard the joke about the skunk?

A You don't want to — it really stinks!

Q How does a cat greet a mouse?

A "Pleased to eat you!"

Q What's the best food to eat on a roller coaster?

A Scream cheese!

Q Why did the cookie go to the doctor?

A Because it was feeling crummy!

Q Why did the golfer bring several pairs of pants?

A In case he got a hole in one!

Q What kind of mouse can jump higher than a house?

A Any kind — a house can't jump!

Q What time is it when an elephant sits on your watch?

A Time to get a new watch!

Q What is a frog's favorite year?

A Leap year!

Q Why shouldn't you tell jokes to an egg?

A Because it might crack up!

Don't miss any of my other fabumouse adventures!

#1 Lost Treasure of the Emerald Eye

#2 The Curse of the Cheese Pyramid

#3 Cat and Mouse in a Haunted House

#4 I'm Too Fond of My Fur!

#5 Four Mice Deep in the Jungle

#6 Paws Off, Cheddarface!

#7 Red Pizzas for a Blue Count

#8 Attack of the Bandit Cats

#9 A Fabumouse Vacation for Geronimo

#10 All Because of a Cup of Coffee

#11 It's Halloween, You 'Fraidy Mouse!

#12 Merry Christmas, Geronimo!

#13 The Phantom of the Subway

#14 The Temple of the Ruby of Fire

#15 The Mona Mousa Code

#16 A Cheese-Colored Camper

#17 Watch Your Whiskers, Stilton!

#18 Shipwreck on the Pirate Islands

#19 My Name Is Stilton, Geronimo Stilton

#20 Surf's Up, Geronimo!

#21 The Wild, Wild West

#22 The Secret of Cacklefur Castle

A Christmas Tale

#23 Valentine's Day Disaster

#24 Field Trip to Niagara Falls

#25 The Search for Sunken Treasure

#26 The Mummy with No Name

#27 The Christmas Toy Factory

#28 Wedding Crasher

#29 Down and Out Down Under

#30 The Mouse Island Marathon

#31 The Mysterious Cheese Thief

Christmas Catastrophe

#32 Valley of the Giant Skeletons

#33 Geronimo and the Gold Medal Mystery

#34 Geronimo Stilton, Secret Agent

#35 A Very Merry Christmas

#36 Geronimo's Valentine

#37 The Race Across America

#38 A Fabumouse
chool Adventure

#39 Singing
Sensation

#40 The Karate
Mouse

#41 Mighty
Mount
Kilimanjaro

#42 The Peculiar
Pumpkin Thief

#43 I'm Not a
Supermouse!

#44 The Giant
Diamond Robbery

#45 Save the
White Whale!

#46 The Haunted
Castle

#47 Run for the
Hills, Geronimo!

48 The Mystery
in Venice

#49 The Way of
the Samurai

#50 This Hotel Is
Haunted

#51 The
Enormouse Pearl
Heist

#52 Mouse in
Space!

#53 Rumble in
the Jungle

#54 Get into
Gear, Stilton!

#55 The Golden
Statue Plot

#56 Flight of the
Red Bandit

The Hunt for the
Golden Book

MEET GERONIMO STILTONIX

He is a spacemouse — the Geronimo Stilton of a parallel universe! He is captain of the spaceship *MouseStar 1*. While flying through the cosmos, he visits distant planets and meets crazy aliens. His adventures are out of this world!

#1 Alien Escape

#2 You're Mine, Captain!

Don't miss these exciting Thea Sisters adventures!

Thea Stilton and the Dragon's Code

Thea Stilton and the Mountain of Fire

Thea Stilton and the Ghost of the Shipwreck

Thea Stilton and the Secret City

Thea Stilton and the Mystery in Paris

Thea Stilton and the Cherry Blossom Adventure

Thea Stilton and the Star Castaways

Thea Stilton: Big Trouble in the Big Apple

Thea Stilton and the Ice Treasure

Thea Stilton and the Secret of the Old Castle

Thea Stilton and the Blue Scarab Hunt

Thea Stilton and the Prince's Emerald

Thea Stilton and the Mystery on the Orient Express

Thea Stilton and the Dancing Shadows

Thea Stilton and the Legend of the Fire Flowers

Thea Stilton and the Spanish Dance Mission

Thea Stilton and the Journey to the Lion's Den

Thea Stilton and the Great Tulip Heist

Thea Stilton and the Chocolate Sabotage

Be sure to read all our magical special edition adventures!

THE KINGDOM OF FANTASY

THE QUEST FOR PARADISE:
THE RETURN TO THE KINGDOM OF FANTASY

THE AMAZING VOYAGE:
THE THIRD ADVENTURE IN THE KINGDOM OF FANTASY

THE DRAGON PROPHECY:
THE FOURTH ADVENTURE IN THE KINGDOM OF FANTASY

THE VOLCANO OF FIRE:
THE FIFTH ADVENTURE IN THE KINGDOM OF FANTASY

THEA STILTON: THE JOURNEY TO ATLANTIS

THEA STILTON: THE SECRET OF THE FAIRIES

Join me and my friends on a journey through time in this very special edition!

THE JOURNEY
THROUGH TIME

Meet
GERONIMO STILTONOOT

He is a cavemouse—Geronimo Stilton's ancient ancestor! He runs the stone newspaper in the prehistoric village of Old Mouse City. From dealing with dinosaurs to dodging meteorites, his life in the Stone Age is full of adventure!

#1 The Stone of Fire #2 Watch Your Tail! #3 Help, I'm in Hot Lava!

#4 The Fast and the Frozen #5 The Great Mouse Race

Meet
CREEPELLA VON CACKLEFUR

I, *Geronimo Stilton*, have a lot of mouse friends, but none as **spooky** as my friend CREEPELLA VON CACKLEFUR! She is an enchanting and MYSTERIOUS mouse with a pet bat named **Bitewing**. YIKES! I'm a real 'fraidy mouse, but even I think CREEPELLA and her family are AWFULLY fascinating. I can't wait for you to read all about CREEPELLA in these fa-mouse-ly funny and **spectacularly spooky** tales!

#1 The Thirteen Ghosts

#2 Meet Me in Horrorwood

#3 Ghost Pirate Treasure

#4 Return of the Vampire

#5 Fright Night

#6 Ride for Your Life

ABOUT THE AUTHOR

Born in New Mouse City, Mouse Island, **GERONIMO STILTON** is Rattus Emeritus of Mousomorphic Literature and of Neo-Ratonic Comparative Philosophy. For the past twenty years, he has been running *The Rodent's Gazette,* New Mouse City's most widely read daily newspaper.

Stilton was awarded the Ratitzer Prize for his scoops on *The Curse of the Cheese Pyramid* and *The Search for Sunken Treasure.* He has also received the Andersen 2000 Prize for Personality of the Year. One of his bestsellers won the 2002 eBook Award for world's best ratlings' electronic book. His works have been published all over the globe.

In his spare time, Mr. Stilton collects antique cheese rinds and plays golf. But what he most enjoys is telling stories to his nephew Benjamin.

1. Main entrance
2. Printing presses (where the books and newspaper are printed)
3. Accounts department
4. Editorial room (where the editors, illustrators, and designers work)
5. Geronimo Stilton's office
6. Helicopter landing pad

THE RODENT'S GAZETTE

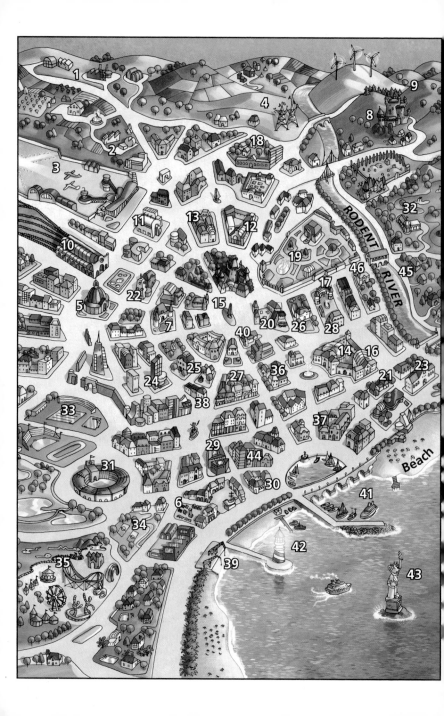

Map of New Mouse City

Map of Mouse Island

Dear mouse friends,
Thanks for reading, and farewell
till the next book.
It'll be another whisker-licking-good
adventure, and that's a promise!

Geronimo Stilton